Copyright 2023

THE DIM BENEATH THE LIGHTS

A pictureword illustrated novella

by R. Overwater

Illustrated by Tom Bagley

This story in its original form first appeared in the anthology Burnt, published by Analemma Books

Hiram had been kneeling in the ashes, doing nothing for a good long while now. Not working, not thinking, just staring at the dark globe half-buried in the scorched ground. Exhaustion hung on him like wet clothing. He needed sleep, and he wasn't getting any under the glare of the damned northern lights.

He shook himself—as if the weariness would just fall away—and tried to figure which direction the sphere might have come from. Ahead, the charred corpse of a deer lay among the burnt trees, trapped by the inferno that erupted when the orb struck. There was no birdsong, no wind rustling through leaves, only dead stillness.

Beyond the trees, Addlestein muttered towards the sky, waving a pencil in one hand, a journal in the other.

Hiram blew on the sphere, smelling his own breath as fog condensed on its cool surface. When he polished it away, his warped reflection stared back at him. Brown and pitted, tobacco-stained where they weren't black with decay, his teeth were rotted by whiskey and molasses. How could any proper lady—a lady like Sarah

Bethany—kiss a filthy pie-hole like that?

He resolved to see one of those tooth doctors when he and Addlestein got the orbs down south.

It would cost plenty, but he'd get a good one, the kind you only found in the big city. Sarah would help.

"Is it another one or not?" a hoarse voice shouted over the thump of approaching hoof beats.

It was Addlestein. Hiram didn't look up. He could see the man's reflection as he rode closer, distorted in the globe's smooth sheen.

"Well?" Addlestein shouted. "Is it?"

"Sorry, Boss," Hiram answered. "My mind keeps wandering."

Addlestein opened his mouth to issue another indignant prompt.

Hiram cut him off. "It's sunk in pretty deep, 'bout the size of a man's head. Cool to the touch, just like the others."

Addlestein dismounted, hobbling through a patch of blackened tree stumps. Puffs of fine ash billowed with each step. Out of habit, Hiram covered his mouth.

Addlestein leaned over Hiram's shoulder. "Well, I'll be damned. It is a big one." He coughed, spitting out a bloody clot.

Hiram looked up. "You sound worse. Can't hardly make out what you're saying."

The older man scowled. "Don't concern yourself. There's a pen and ink in my saddlebag. Put the orb with the others and mark an 'X' on the catalog page. I'll note its properties when we make camp." He shot Hiram a self-satisfied smile. "I'd leave it to you, if you could write more than your own name."

Stuck-up bastard. Lording over Hiram every chance he got. Sarah was teaching him to read and write. Soon, sons-of-bitches like Addlestein wouldn't always have the upper hand.

Bankers and businessmen, they didn't work any harder than Hiram did. They weren't any stronger, couldn't shoot any straighter, couldn't ride any harder. They pissed standing up no different than him. But they had power—power that came from words on paper. If you could read those words, make your own words, you could hold their kind of power. If you had that, all you needed was a good shave and a clean suit.

Hiram was going to get those things. Sarah had promised. But first, he needed to get Addlestein down to California and meet the men coming west from the Smithsonian museum. By Addlestein's account, the Smithsonian men had found an orb in some tar pit and were eager to compare it to his—and they were willing to pay.

Getting paid meant keeping Addlestein alive until then. Hiram wondered if the man would even make it out of Alaska. He looked like hell. Every time he spoke, it triggered a coughing fit. A yellow, flaking rash covered his skin and he scratched at it constantly.

Hiram was starting to show the wear of hard living too. He'd seen that in the orb's reflection. After years on the trail, driving cattle, escorting settlers, any job he could find—and then gambling and drinking his pay away—it was time to put that all behind him. He needed to make sure this opportunity didn't slip by.

Some opportunity. If he'd known what he was in for when Sarah read him the newspaper advertisement, he might have said no.

"Wanted for immediate hire," she said, looking over the edge of the nickel paper to see if he was listening. "Experienced trail hand to accompany scientific expedition. Salary commensurate with length of journey."

Sarah urged him to reply. She needed the money to build them a better life and, hopefully, Hiram would make a name for himself, bringing him closer to the fancy world she missed so much. She had plans and he was lucky to be the man who would make them happen.

Addlestein paid well. If Hiram spent it on barbers, tailors and new teeth, he'd be civilized enough for Sarah's purposes.

He marked the catalog, packed the orb away and saddled up. The two men rode until they were back among living trees. It was late when they pitched camp.

Afterwards, Hiram finally worked up the nerve to ask Addlestein about the lights.

Every night, he'd lay awake. Above, a writhing canopy of pink and green spread to the horizon. Long streaks of white slid through the glimmering colors, hissing like burning snakes. They were bright enough to read by, not that Hiram could read. But he did know such a grand display was uncommon before winter. Knowing more might dampen his uneasiness. He should have kept his mouth shut.

"Ah-roar-ah..."

"Aurora borealis," Addlestein said, finishing Hiram's sentence with trademark disdain. "Most natives up here think they're animal spirits or some such." The firelight colored his skin a sickly orange. "Some Eskimos think they're evil. The Fox Indians think they're slain enemies seeking revenge."

It was all horseshit. The boss wasn't just ill, he was crazy. There'd been plenty of examples, like that very night when they made camp.

Hiram had gone into the trees to gather firewood. When he returned, Addlestein jammed a map in his face, tapping a line of dots circled on it. "Equidistant across the longitude and parallel to the latitude!" he shouted, laughing, limping back and forth. He spat, and then laughed again.

"And this!" He held up his journal, a crude calendar scribbled on one page. "Another will fall close to here this very week." He wandered away, shaking his fistful of paper, shouting as if someone was there to hear.

Addlestein spooked Hiram almost as much as the lights did. When he laid out his bedroll, he tucked his pistol inside it.

Squirming on the hard ground until he found the right position between the rocks and lumps, he pulled out his worn picture of Sarah. He kept it folded so it fit his pocket, and a jagged crease now divided her into two halves. Hiram never noticed, his mind forming a complete image of her whenever he held it.

He squinted at the photograph until Addlestein's coughing interrupted his thoughts. Watching him lie with his back to the fire, hacking and clawing at his skin, Hiram considered the cards life had dealt the retired schoolmaster. One of the only survivors in a town razed to the ground after the first orb fell, his family dead... Hiram saw how a man could go half mad.

Addlestein said his quest was in the name of science. Probably, he was just trying to play a bad hand as best he could.

When he awoke later that night, Hiram's throat burned from smoke. It happened sometimes when the campfire needed stoking. Except it wasn't their fire. A short distance from the camp, flames roared through the willow branches.

He leapt up and scanned the clearing, worried the horses might bolt. But Addlestein was tending to them at the clearing's edge. He had one already saddled and stood half mounted, a foot in one stirrup, using his vantage point to peer through the flames.

When Hiram caught his eye, he pointed into the fire. "I saw it!" he yelled. "I saw it come down and land over there!"

They had to wait until late next evening for the blaze to subside and the smoke to clear. Addlestein found it first.

"Look," he whispered as Hiram walked up. It was almost three quarters sunken into the ground, about as round as a small washbasin. Its surface rippled with color, as if the northern lights were inside it.
Addlestein reached down hesitantly, feeling it with his palm. He emitted a strangled gasp. "Touch it."

Poking it with a fingertip, Hiram jumped back. He could feel the hot ground through his boot soles. Sweat dripped from the faces of both men. Yet, despite having fallen from above and igniting hundreds of yards of bush, the orb was icy to the touch. Not just cool like the others—cold as a frozen pond.

He could see Addlestein had no explanation. Hiram looked at the eerie luminescence above their heads. The end of this ride couldn't come soon enough.

They rode for another month, following the path scrawled on Addlestein's map. By now, Hiram was packing all the supplies. Addlestein, protective of his prizes from the start, insisted on carrying the orbs himself. With the latest one, his horse couldn't bear any more weight.

They found one more. It was shiny silver, glinting in the noonday sun, maybe six feet across judging by the few inches of curved surface above ground. Addlestein clutched his head, murmuring, agonizing over what to do.

They had no choice but to bury it. Addlestein pulled out his map and compass, carefully noting their location. There was hope in his eyes when Hiram returned from stowing the spade.

"The Smithsonian will pay a tidy sum when we return for this one," he said. He spat a glob of ash-black saliva. "Whatever fortunes we make on this trip, we are poised to double that."

Hiram stayed quiet. They were never coming back this way.

The next day, the sky filled with dark, swirling clouds and a thunderstorm hammered them with rain shortly after sunset. They hunkered down near a stand of pines, doing their best to keep dry. Hiram was cold and wet, but grateful the clouds obscured the aurora's glow. It was the darkest night so far, illuminated only by lightning flashes. He thought he might get some sleep, when a movement caught the corner of his eye.

He ran to his pack and dug for his pistol. "Boss!"

"What?" Addlestein shouted, visibly alarmed.

"I thought there was... look." Hiram pointed toward the tarpaulin covering the saddles and packs.

The tarpaulin bucked like something alive, and the sacks rolled from beneath them, tumbling on the wet ground. The one with the two largest globes careened off Addlestein, hurling him into the mud.

Hiram pulled out his Barlow knife and looked at Addlestein, who nodded. Keeping his distance, he danced around the shifting sacks, slashing at them. The orbs spilled out and instantly smacked together in a tight clump. He stood back and let out a low whistle.

"I wonder..." Addlestein said, getting to his feet. He took Hiram's knife and approached the cluster. The knife leapt from his fingers and clacked against the largest one, clinging tightly.

Then they were blind. Lightning shot down, engulfing the spheres in blue sparks. The men stumbled back, slipping and falling in the mud. Their ears rang from the thunder crack and the tang of ozone burned their nostrils.

Hiram and Addlestein lay there in the mud. The rain continued to beat down.

The orbs' grip relaxed and they settled apart, rolling to accommodate the uneven ground. Addlestein rose, blinking to regain his vision, and nudged one with his foot. "Whatever phenomenon we just witnessed, it now appears to be over."

Hiram rubbed his muddy hands on his pant legs. "For a minute, I figured we were gonna have a hard time sacking 'em up again ."

They rode into Skagway two weeks before the SS Aleutian embarked for San Francisco. The first night, Hiram drew the hotel room curtains and vowed to never again underestimate the pleasure of sleeping in darkness.

Addlestein sold the horses and spent his days sending telegrams and making arrangements. Reluctantly, he helped Hiram telegraph Miss Sarah Bethany and arrange for her to come north and meet them.

Hiram was elated, and treated himself to a bath every day. He'd seen a barber immediately and spent a chunk of his next advance on a tan suit and patent leather shoes. At the tailor's advice, he'd picked a red silk kerchief to tuck into the breast pocket. It was the first suit he'd ever owned. Wearing it was like being hogtied.

"Good lord, Hiram." Sarah put her hand to her mouth when she saw him on the station platform. "Your skin is practically falling off your bones." She caught herself, softening her expression. Setting her case and parasol down, she stepped closer and touched his lapel.

"But look at you! Proper attire and grooming! Without any help whatsoever."

She pressed up, draping her arms loosely around his neck. Hiram leaned in to peck her on the lips. She turned slightly, letting it fall on her cheek. It was disappointing but he figured she needed to keep up appearances.

It also wouldn't do for a proper woman like Sarah to bunk with a man she wasn't married to. Hiram had seen her logic in that. Even though he ached to lie beside her, he could wait. He'd booked her hotel room close to his anyways.

With Addlestein's help, he secured a table at the hotel restaurant—the kind of place that normally wouldn't allow someone like him through the door. He did his best to mimic Sarah as she ate in measured bites. It was all he could do to keep from shoveling it in; after months of pemmican and molasses, it was the best food he'd ever tasted.

After the meal, over steaming cups of dark coffee, she beamed at him, reaching out and touching the back of his hand as he recounted his trip and described their strange cargo.

"We've done it, Hiram, exactly as we hoped we could." Her green eyes looked deep into his. "We're at the forefront of a scientific discovery, one that will astound the world." Hiram felt a grin spreading across his face.

"From here, our futures are assured," she continued. "With my education and—" the corners of her mouth barely dropped—"the respectable man a woman needs, we are all set."

Hiram crawled into his comfortable bed after they parted, imagining Sarah Bethany in her bedclothes only a few rooms away. He drifted off, pleased with himself.

In the morning, Addlestein joined them for breakfast before they boarded the passenger liner. Sarah had no end of questions for him: several about the orbs and a few about seeking recognition.

"No, actually," he answered, looking thoughtful. "I hadn't thought about the newspapers. A story would certainly enhance my stature as a discoverer, wouldn't it?"

Sarah didn't respond. Hiram could tell she was staring at the sores on his cheeks. Addlestein could tell also, blushing slightly.

"And Hiram's stature as an able man in the field," she said finally. "Don't forget the seasoned trail hand whose skills helped precipitate this amazing discovery."

"Yes, yes," Addlestein answered, looking away as he dragged his nails down one arm. "It would have been impossible without an extra man."

Breakfast was quiet after that. Miss Bethany said nothing as they went back to their rooms and waited for the bellhop to come for their belongings

On the deck of the Aleutian, Hiram ignored the unsteady, rolling sensation and marveled at the sight of receding land, the bustling harbor and busy ships.

Sarah took him by the elbow as they strolled the length of the promenade. "That man has some sort of consumption, and is most surely in denial," she said. "He will never speak before the prominent scientific community." She turned, stopping them where they stood. "He is dreadful. They will separate him from his discovery as soon as they can."

Hiram thought about it. Addlestein, watching his home and family burn, riding hell-bent every day through miles of devastated forest, chasing the things that had cost him his whole world. And then getting cut out of the deal that could bring his story full circle, offer some sort of redemption.

Sarah was peering into his eyes. "It will happen, despite the fact he is an articulate, learned man," she said. "When we dock in California, I will contract a photographer to capture us with the spheres."

Before Hiram could answer, she pressed on. "His ego will allow this. Then we'll contact the press and your name will be synonymous with these discoveries. What he does after that, successful or not, will matter little to us."

Hiram was unsure, but he felt her excitement. He was too sheepish to ask what synonymous meant.

Addlestein all but collapsed at dinner the first night. Sarah, God bless her, saw him to his room and offered to spend the trip caring for him.

It made sense the way she explained it. "You worked so hard to get him here and our futures depend on him," she said. She put her arms around Hiram, squeezing him. "You've earned some leisure. The least I can do is this."

His nights unexpectedly free, Hiram found himself at the poker table. He'd forgotten how strong its call used to be, but he remembered now. He had enough money left to ride the ebb and flow of luck and, by the time they closed the gambling tables, he'd pocketed a good haul. Enough to buy something nice for Sarah.

Rising late the next morning, he shook off the previous evening's liquor and got right back at it. The cards liked Hiram. They were telling him that Miss Bethany was right, that this trip really was a new beginning. It occurred to him: he should squirrel away some money for a ring.

"You got the winning touch there, pard," a voice said over his shoulder as he made his way back from the water closet. Hiram turned to see a clean-cut man in his early thirties. He wore a white uniform with gold insignia on his chest.

Hiram remembered him; he'd seen him speaking to the captain before the Aleutian shoved off.

"I know a winner when I see one and I'm sitting on a good stake because of it," the crewman said. He looked around, then leaned in close. "'Course, it's no good for the bos'n to be seen gambling on duty."

"I suppose it ain't," Hiram said. "But, might be your captain won't mind you buying a man a drink." The bosun smiled and slapped Hiram's shoulder, motioning toward the bar.

His name was Dupris, and he'd obviously been doing this for a while. He saw Hiram as a winner and, hell, that's exactly what he was now.

Hiram spent the rest of the afternoon and all that night betting big, sometimes losing big, but mostly winning big.

He was so focused on the cards, he didn't notice the room growing slowly louder until it was impossible to ignore. When the dealer closed the table for a fifteen-minute recess, Hiram saw that half the crowd had filed out to the deck. He could hear excited voices.

"Lived here all my life, only saw this once," said a woman.

"Absolutely breathtaking," a man's voice answered.

Hiram's stomach dropped when he set foot on the deck. Everyone was staring skyward. Looking up, he could arrive at only one thought: the lights were following him.

The crowd gaped at the multi-hued spectacle. They were off the Washington coast by now, still far enough north this sight wasn't unheard of. But rarely was it this intense. Not down here.

They churned and flashed as vividly as they had in Alaska, but the lights didn't extend to the northern horizon. They were right above, reaching for only a few miles. Suddenly sober, Hiram returned to the table, ordered a double whiskey, and asked to be dealt back in.

When he met Dupris in his cabin afterwards, the bosun produced a bottle and poured two fingers of bourbon into a pair of dirty glasses. He handed one over, looking tired. "This is the only good thing to happen today," he said, shaking the handful of bills Hiram had won him. "Compass is off three degrees for some reason, and slowly getting worse."

He gulped back the drink and reached for the bottle. "Captain made me spend the whole shift double-checking our navigator. Had to account for the drift. Not even my job."

Hiram only half listened. Despite his best efforts, his mind was elsewhere. The sky outside had put a knot in his gut and all the whiskey he drank that night—a lot of whiskey—couldn't untie it.

Dupris was still talking, and Hiram made like he'd been listening. Dupris winked. "With a stack like yours, I can introduce you to a couple ladies who'll gladly take your company. Not dance hall girls. Real ladies."

It hit him: he hadn't seen Sarah for nearly two days. "I got a lady," Hiram said. He downed his drink and started for the door. He stopped and looked over his shoulder. "Thanks."

It was late. He wondered if Sarah would forgive him for waking her, but something already had. She leaned against the cabin doorframe, speaking to a tall porter.

"Hiram!" Sarah shoved past the porter, leaping on him. "I didn't know where you were. I've been terrified."

Her cheeks were flushed and Hiram felt the moist heat of her skin through her nightdress.

The porter was still there, looking awkward, and she waved him away. She seized Hiram's wrist. "I fled that awful Mr. Addlestein a few hours ago," she said, closing the door behind them. "He's lost his mind."

Sarah loosened her collar, tugging it down a few inches, giving him a tantalizing glimpse of the uppermost portion of one breast. A purple welt bloomed above it.

"Do you see this? I tried to care for him, since he's clearly at death's door. But in his delirium, he's so jealous." She put one hand to her mouth. "He accused me of trying to smother him! Said we are conspiring against him!"

Sarah blinked, tears welling. "If he hadn't been in a weakened state when he attacked..." She let the words hang.

Hiram's thoughts went black. He pushed Sarah away, fighting to check his anger. The mad bastard had finally gone too far. She sat on the rumpled bed, reading his grim expression.

Her voice was quiet when she finally spoke. "Do you still have your pistol?"

Hiram knocked once on the painted steel of Addlestein's cabin door, and then turned the door handle. It wrenched itself out of his grasp, as if someone pulled it from the other side. But no one was standing there. The tension lingering in his gut coiled tighter.

The door refused to open more than halfway and Hiram squeezed around it, pistol leveled at waist height. Before he got through, the gun jumped from his hand, banging against two steamer trunks in the corner, clinging to the side of one. Other metal objects—coins, a money clip, scissors—were stuck to the trunks as well.

A wet cough cut through the hum of the steamship. Addlestein's bed was in the corner opposite the trunks. Propped against the headboard, he peered over a grimy bed sheet, red-rimmed eyes punctuating a face more open sores than flesh. He convulsed, choking as he clawed at his skin. The sheet fell away and Hiram flinched at the sight.

Long fingernail grooves tracked down what little skin remained, most of it scraped away in desperate fits of itching. The sheets were stained red, bits of raw flesh stuck to them, and strands of hair lay fallen from a now bare, pocked scalp. Hiram had seen dead bodies before. Few looked as bad as this still-living man.

Addlestein raised a shaking hand, crooking one finger towards the pile of metal in the corner, voice barely more than a whisper. "These aren't accidental creations of nature. They are artifacts of unknown design."

For a moment, there was light behind the swollen vessels in his eyes. "Otherworldly perhaps. In the last two days..." He coughed. "...intermittently magnetic, right to the exact hour."

Hiram knew what magnetism was. And he understood now why the ship's compass was off.

He stepped toward the bed. Addlestein nodded weakly, half smiling. "Yes, yes. You've come to finish what she failed to complete herself."

Hiram struggled to make sense of what he was saying. Sarah never could have—

"It's alright, Hiram," Addlestein coughed. "We

both know I'm finished. Take them. Seek your fortune."
His back arched as he fought another round of spasms. It was a full minute before he continued. "I see it now—they emanate some undetectable, poisonous quality. You're lucky it was I who was packing them. This..." He looked down at his body. "This is what you'll inherit."

Addlestein was uppity, ornery, a horse's ass. He looked down his nose at Hiram, ordered him about as he pleased, and left him all the backbreaking work. But he was not a liar or a cheat. Hiram had rode with the man. What he knew about him didn't square up with Sarah's story. Or what she wanted Hiram to do to him.

He could hardly believe Addlestein's accusations about her, either. He wrestled with the contradiction.

A woman like Sarah would surely value a man with some backbone. He would insist on finishing the job and see Addlestein to California like he'd been paid to. The wretch was as good as dead anyways and their plans would unfold without a shot fired. She'd see the wisdom.

Hiram got his next steps straight in his mind. "Here's how it's gonna be," he said. Before he could finish, the items hugging the steamer trunks clattered to the floor. He heard Addlestein inhale, saw his eyes go wide in amazement.

Right then, Hiram saw the purity of Addlestein's obsession. The old schoolmaster burned with curiosity right to the end, knowing the orbs were killing him. Knowing he would never see their mystery explained. There was a difference between the thing that drove him and the motivations of Sarah and Hiram.

The ship lurched, throwing him down on all fours. The room tilted, pictures fell from the wall and the steamer trunks and loose articles slid toward him in an avalanche of debris. A deep metallic groan shuddered through the compartment, through Hiram's bones, and the clang of bells pierced the cabin walls.

Voices rose outside, and through the half-open door Hiram saw people flooding into the passageway. "We've run aground," a panicked woman yelled.

"Ladies and gentlemen, proceed to the upper main deck," a deeper, authoritarian voice shouted.

The orbs could sink into the mud for all Hiram cared. He'd never learn what they were, where they came from, same as Addlestein. The difference was, he didn't give a damn.

He pushed himself up, noticing the pistol sliding towards him. He caught it and a shot rang out.

A red hole blossomed in Addlestein's chest and he rolled off the bed, face slack, a final pink bubble on his lips.

Hiram looked at his pistol. Impossible. How could he have—a second shot boomed and pain tore though Hiram's skull, blinding him, thrusting him face-first to the floor.

He strained to move his limbs. They were as dead as burnt timber. Around him he heard shuffling sounds. Blood stung his eyes and he blinked until he made out shadowy forms.

Two men carried Addlestein's trunks, one atop the other.

There, by the door, was Sarah, a pistol in one hand. The other hand rested on the cheek of the tall porter. She handed him the pistol and he tucked it inside his coat, turning for the door. The men with the trunks followed.

Sarah remained still for a moment, looking around the room, scratching at her neck. She approached Hiram, leaned over, and looked deep into his eyes. There was no denying it; she thought he was dead.

"Sarah," he tried to call out. She looked for another moment, then went to the desk and rummaged through the drawers.

"Ah!" she said, raising Addlestein's journal. Stuffing it under her arm, she left, pulling the door tight behind her.

Hiram tried to call out again, hard as he could. Only a gasp emerged. The agony in his skull grew stronger above one ear. Sticky wetness pooled around his face.

The door pushed open again. Something gray and filmy crowded the edges of his vision but he could tell it was Sarah. She'd heard him after all.

His heart leapt as she leaned down, touching his chest. He felt his jacket open and she pulled out the wad of poker earnings.

Then she strode back to the door, pausing to look into the hallway. In the dimming light, on the back of her neck, red lines showed where her fingernails had broken the skin.

--END--

www.overwater.ca

This book was written and drawn by humans. No artificial intelligence was used in its creation. No intelligence at all, actually.

Printed in the USA
CPSIA information can be obtained
at www.ICGtesting.com
JSHW070733140124
55335JS00015B/28